HOMECOMING

Karma Police Book Six

SEAN PLATT

DAVID W. WRIGHT

STERLING & STONE

HOMECOMING

HOMECOMING

Chapter One

Ella

～

THE DOOR EXPLODES off its hinges, men and women in black uniforms — AD agents — storm in with guns on us.

Outside our room, chaos: gunshots and screams, as Fairchild's men attack the underground headquarters, shooting indiscriminately.

This is a war, and the enemy body count means nothing.

The First Front has lost, and now they've come for the general's surrender.

Ben looks at me, tears and blame in his eyes like I purposely led them here. Like I betrayed him.

But then, as he drops his gun with a sigh, I see that the true emotion is fear. I can't help but wonder if this is one of the dark visions he'd seen in Eden's memories, now coming true. And I wonder how much I'm to blame.

"Down on your knees, hands on your head!" yells one of the agents, his rifle going back and forth between Ben and me.

We do as we're told, me taking a bit more time in this old man's body. A second agent, a short woman with a severe crew cut, instructs us to put our hands behind our backs then proceeds to cuff us. She then steps in front of us, looks down, speaking into a com on her shoulder, "Big fish and little fish are secure."

I look at Ben, wondering why he's not fighting back. He can send a shock to their minds, incapacitate them and allow us time to escape.

But he's not doing anything.

That's when I notice him gritting his teeth like he's in pain.

Moments later, Fairchild steps into the tiny dark room wearing his perfectly pressed, spotless suit, with the same red tie and rose like always, looking like a dapper version of an armchair general coming to collect his spoils now that the real fighting is done.

And then I see why Ben isn't fighting back.

Irina is behind Fairchild, dressed in the AD agent-issued black uniform, her long black hair accentuated with a crimson strand, either an extension or coloring. She's focused on him, obviously exerting her psychic grip, preventing him from using his power.

She looks at Ben. "Where's Nikolai?"

Ben looks at her, shaking his head. "He's not here, Irina. He's in a safe place where *he* can't get to him."

Ben says *he* while barely nodding toward Fairchild, as if he can't even look directly at the man.

Irina steps forward, draws her gun, aims it at Ben, then practically growls, "Where is he?"

"You kill me, and you'll never see him again. I don't know what story he sold you, but I'm *protecting* Niko. Did Fairchild tell you what he plans to do with your brother? Did he?"

"Shut up with your lies!" she yells, gun trembling in her hand.

Fairchild, perhaps sensing that the girl is about to snap and maybe kill Ben, steps toward her. He gently sets his hand on her gun and lowers it. "It's okay, Irina. We'll find your brother. It's only a matter of time."

Fairchild looks at me.

My mind is still reeling from everything that's happened, particularly the revelation that I'm not who I thought I was. Nor what I thought I was. Something — like the man I thought was my father said — *new.*

I think of the colorful energy that Ben saw leave Eden's body following the car crash. Was that me? And if so, which me? Willow? Ella? Eden? And where have I been the past five years? A half-decade of blank memories following my time in Irina's body.

But now that Ben has uploaded all of these old memories into me, belonging to him, Willow, Eden, and to Ella — the person I thought I was — I can't just shut them off. I can't just be whoever or whatever it is that I'm supposed to be.

I only know who I feel like — Ella.

And because I have Ella's history, every fiber of whatever I am hates Fairchild. I hate him for what he did to Ben's father. I hate him for what he did to me — or, rather, Ella. I hate him for what he's about to do to the world if he finds Niko.

We can't let that happen.

I have to figure a way out of this, but how can I do

anything when I'm trapped in the body of Clifton Emmanuel, a 65-year-old man known as The Fixer, a glorified handyman working for The First Front? Even if I could tap into any of the fighting or weapons skills I've collected on my journey, my body is old. They'll kill me before I can get off my knees.

Maybe that's the secret? Maybe if I can get myself killed, whatever is controlling me will guide me into another, better body?

I don't know who or what is controlling me these past several years, but I don't think it was Ben or The First Front. They have a couple of Jumpers, but Ben was as surprised to see me here as Fairchild was when I wound up in one of his agents.

But as I consider lunging at Irina, who is closest to me, I can't help but hesitate. I'm not sure if it'll even work. So far, every time I've fallen asleep, passed out, or gotten killed, I manage to wake up in a different body, but there's no guarantee. And I can't just throw Clifton's life away. As long as I've been Jumping, I've lived by the motto, *Do Not Interfere and Always Leave Someone's Life a Bit Better Than You Found It.*

I can't just get him killed.

Fairchild steps toward us, lording over the moment, over his immense power, holding our lives in his hands.

I wonder if he knows that I know what I am. If that would matter. I figure it is best that he keeps thinking whatever he already thinks, at least long enough to give me some advantage I can't yet see.

He looks at Ben, "Why? Why have you been so hard at work screwing up our Karma missions?"

Ben says nothing. Just looks down at the ground.

Fairchild shakes his head. "Willow would be so disappointed in you, turning on your own like this."

Ben doesn't rise to the bait.

"Well, here's the good news, Benjamin. I haven't given up on you yet."

He turns and leaves. As he does, he tells his agents, "Put them in the van and bring them home."

Home?

Chapter Two

Ben

~

I'M in the back of the van, hands cuffed behind me, as we drive "home," which I'm assuming is Advanced Dynamics.

Willow's beside me, holding my hand, squeezing it, saying, "It's going to be okay."

I smile and say, "I know," even though I'm not sure I believe it.

Clifton, inhabited by the thing that thinks of itself as my daughter, is looking at me. "Who are you talking to?"

I shake my head. "Nobody."

I don't explain for two reasons. One, how to explain to someone that some part of Willow lives on inside of me, one last gift from Eden before she returned to AD? Then we'd have to get into the whole discussion of whether or not she's real or just some projection in my head. And hell, *I* don't even know what's real anymore. All I know is that she's there for me, and right now I need her — whatever part of her is left in this world.

The second reason is that I don't want anyone else to know that part of Willow lives on inside of me. Her father, Fairchild, would not be happy, and would likely do everything in his power to take her away. Take what's left and put her into another of his cyborg monstrosities.

So I keep her my secret.

Ella, in Clifton's body, goes back to staring at the van floor, probably lost in some existential crisis of learning that she isn't who she thought. Or maybe she's trying to find a way out of this, like me.

Willow looks at Clifton, then back at me. "You know she didn't lead them to you. At least not on purpose."

I know, I think, rather than speak.

The stabbing pain in my head is back.

I cry out.

Willow flickers, then she's gone.

It's Irina. Squelching my powers from behind the metal partition separating the front and back of the van, trying to keep from escaping. Now and then she finds a weakness in my psychic walls and tries to batter it down, so she can worm inside my head, and find her brother.

I focus on the metal partition, sealing the hole, and the pain fades to a low roar.

I'm not sure how long I can keep her out. If I could just get to her, either with a physical or psychic attack of my own, I could disable whatever signal she uses to keep me weak.

Then I could access the van's electrical system and crash it.

Or incapacitate the agents, and escape.

My only hope is to wait until Irina tires.

But if that doesn't happen by the time we reach AD,

I'm screwed. They'll put me in The Cage — a deep underground cell where escape is impossible.

Once there, I'm stuck until they either kill me or let me go.

As if there are two options.

Fairchild will never let me go. Once he has what he wants, he'll kill me — just like he did my father. I'm an enemy now, and enemies can reveal secrets to the world, get AD shut down, or at the very least, de-funded. The government hates when someone shines a light on their secret programs.

I wonder how many of my people they've killed or captured in the raid. Did anyone else escape?

Am I all that's left?

I had twenty-five people in The First Front, making me directly responsible for twenty-five lives, nineteen of them Deviants. Twenty-five people who trusted me and bought into my war against AD, who believed in fighting tyranny.

And now, unless some of them escaped, they're all either captured or dead. If they're captured, Fairchild will interrogate them, trying to get any information he can on Niko.

But I'm the only one who knows where Niko is, which means these interrogations will be brutal. And once Fairchild realizes they're not going to, or can't, give him what he wants, they're all as good as dead.

Even if he doesn't kill them, they'll never have their lives back. Maybe he'll try to reprogram them. Or imprison them in Aspen Falls.

The only thing I know for certain is that things can't get much worse for any of us. But at least Fairchild won't get to Niko.

He'll hurt me. My interrogation will be the worst. But

I'm not giving him Niko's location. I've prepared for this eventuality ever since I went underground.

I've also created deadly defenses around the information in case he tries to send a Jumper into me.

I don't think Fairchild has any idea about the fight he's in for, or how far I've come in my psychic defenses since we last saw one another.

An idea comes to me.

If I could choke Clifton out, Ella might be able to Jump, and maybe into the body of someone who can help us.

But my hands are cuffed around a metal loop in the floor, keeping me where I am. Ella's hands are similarly bound.

I look at Willow, now back and shaking her head. She looks at Clifton and says, "He could die."

He'd be willing to die to save the world.

She looks at him again, then back at me. "There's got to be another way."

Have you got any ideas? Because I'm just about out, and we're going to be at AD any moment now.

She looks at Clifton, then me, and shakes her head. "No."

"Ella," I say softly, hoping the people up front won't hear me. I'm not sure if Irina can hear us or not. If she can, then we need to act quickly before she puts a stop to this.

Clifton looks up. "Yes?"

"Can you control your Jumps?"

"No."

"But you said you keep Jumping into people involved with what's going on, right?"

"Yes. I think so. But I don't know how. I don't know who my co-pilot is, or if I even have one."

"We've gotta go with what we've got. I need you to knock yourself out."

"How?"

"Hit your head against the wall over and over until you pass out."

"What? I might kill Clifton!"

"If you don't do it, *they* might kill Clifton. And they will definitely kill *you*."

Clifton/Ella swallows.

And then, surprisingly without any more argument, leans forward, then violently thrusts backward, bashing his head into the van with a sickening thud.

My stomach lurches at the sound, at the grimace on Clifton's face as blood spills from his scalp.

He's still conscious.

"Again," I say.

He looks at me, eyes watering.

SMASH!

The van lurches to a stop.

"Shit, they're coming. Keep going!"

Ella smashes her head once, twice more. There's a sickening crunch that reverberates through my body and twists my insides.

The doors launch open, bright light blinding me.

Irina and two agents stand there, staring in shock.

Ella throws her head backward again, but before she can smash Clifton's skull into the wall, she stops mid-movement, frozen.

Irina's hand is sticking straight out, fingers twitching, as if she physically caught Clifton's head in mid-arc. Then she splays her fingers as if pulling his head forward to a stop.

Clifton sits back up, eyes dazed and blinking. Blood is

splattered on the wall behind him, and trickling down his forehead. Surely, he'll pass out, and then Ella can Jump.

"Get the healer here," Irina says into her com.

Moments later, another agent appears — a young blonde named Brianna who went to the school a few years ago.

Brianna looks at me, a sad look in her eyes as if she knows she's betraying me.

"Fix him up, now!" Irina barks.

Brianna lays her hands on the back of Clifton's skull. I've seen her work minor miracles on broken legs and third-degree burns. Surely, a cracked skull won't be difficult to mend.

Irina glares at both me and Ella.

"Nobody's getting out of this until I have my brother."

Chapter Three

Ben

~

I WOKE up on a hard cot about an hour ago in The Cage.

I don't remember being knocked out, nor do I have any idea how long I was unconscious.

The room is silent, except for the rush of blood through my veins and the thrumming heartbeat behind it.

Not the sound of people, nor their machines. No stray radio or wifi. Nothing I can latch on to and send for help. As if there was anyone left to help me now.

Everyone I know is likely either dead or captured by Fairchild's agents.

The Cage was built in the bowels of AD, deep in one of its secret sub-levels, designed to prevent a Deviant from accessing any signals or electronics. Everything operates manually.

I remember when this room was built. Hell, I was

consulted on its construction. "How would you keep someone with your abilities locked up?" Fairchild asked.

Only now, looking back, does it seem so obvious that he was asking how I'd lock *me* up — that he was planning for the inevitable day when the two of us would be enemies. Hell, maybe our looming battle was in one of his visions.

The room is a cold twelve by twelve chamber with bright white walls staring back at me, reflecting a row of battery-operated light panels overhead. There's a heavy vault door which only opens from the outside.

I stare up at the small vent in the ceiling, wishing I could shrink myself and escape.

But there is no escape.

I'm here as long as Fairchild wants me to be. Here as long as he wants me alive.

I wonder how many of my comrades are in similar rooms, being interrogated for information they don't have. I wonder how long before Fairchild comes to torture me.

As if on cue, I hear the tumblers in the vault door slide into place.

I consider standing to attack whoever's coming in, but I know better. Whoever has come for me has taken precautions.

The door slides open.

It's Fairchild himself. And Irina.

I can feel her assault on my brain the moment she enters, paralyzing my limbs.

I get up and try to stand, to move toward them, but my body freezes in a sitting position. Irina has severed my brain's connection to my extremities.

I imagine she's also squelching my ability to fight psychically, so that I won't try anything. Yet.

Fairchild steps in then signals to one of his agents in

black to shut the door. I imagine he's got a secret knock to indicate when to open it again, which limits my ability to escape, even if I could somehow disable both of my tormentors.

I sit up in bed, watching them both, sizing up the situation, looking for any moment to escape.

He steps toward me, a pitying look as if to say, "My boy, how did we ever come to this?"

He stops five feet in front of me, folds his hands and meets my gaze. "I hope the accommodations aren't too uncomfortable, but I'm figuring what with your little war against me, you can understand the ..." he looks around the sterile chamber, "*extreme* precautions."

I just stare at him.

I don't even look at Irina, standing just outside my field of vision, over to my right near the toilet and sink.

"We don't need to be enemies, Ben."

There's one thing on my mind, the accusation that I've wanted to level at him ever since I went into hiding, the secret I learned from Eden.

But I hold it close, for now, because once I say it, I'm not sure I'll be able to gird myself against the emotions that are certain to follow.

Fairchild speaks again, "Where is he?"

"You'll never find him."

Irina practically growls, "Let me at him."

I don't look at her. Not that I'm afraid, though I'd be lying if I said I wasn't, as I'm sure she's only grown in power since the last time I saw her. But mostly I don't look at Irina because I don't want to provoke her.

Irina wants her brother back. I'm not sure what lies Fairchild has filled her head with, but to her, I am the enemy. The one thing keeping her from a reunion with Niko. Whatever remains of that scared little girl that came into my office five years ago seeking help is gone, replaced by an angry young woman desperate for justice.

But I have no fight with her, only the old man smugly smiling like some sinister puppeteer.

Fairchild raises a hand to calm Irina. "No need to let things get ugly, my dear. I'm sure Ben will cooperate. He's not a bad man. He's just confused. He needs to understand the situation better. We can help him."

Irina harrumphs.

Fairchild asks, "What is it that you want with Niko?"

"I think the better question is what do *you* want with him? Have you told AD your plans? Have you told Irina?"

I look at the girl and see the smallest seed of doubt in her eyes. Of course, she tries to hide it.

Fairchild says nothing.

"Did he tell you?" I ask Irina.

She says nothing.

"Okay, well since the cat has both of your tongues, why don't I just tell you. Fairchild is going to use your brother to unleash a psychic virus that will more or less kill everyone."

"Not everyone," Fairchild corrects me. "Just our enemies. The people who want us dead."

"It'll wipe out most of humanity, rendering them more or less braindead. You can't think that's a good idea, Irina. Your brother certainly doesn't. He wants no part of this. He begged me to help him escape."

I look at Irina, still staring me down like she wants to rip me apart. If I'm getting through, I can't tell. Is she even listening to me or does Fairchild have her so brainwashed that every word from my lips is some evil ploy? Her poker face is unflinching, and I have to hope that she's hiding any doubts she might have as a matter of self-preservation.

Fairchild, still looking as calm as he did when he stepped into The Cage, says, "Niko doesn't know what's coming. He doesn't know what they've been doing to our kind. Hell, I don't think you even know, Ben. Are you aware of what's going on in Russia, in Europe?"

He shakes his head as if to pity my ignorance, then keeps right on talking.

"Their Deviant programs have been shut down. And now the governments have been killing us or putting us in camps, just like the Nazis did in World War Two. There *is* a war being fought, and our side is going to lose unless we do something. I've seen the future, Ben. I've seen you, me, Irina, Niko, *all of us Deviants*, rounded up, tortured, experimented on like lab animals. Killed. Humans won't tolerate what they fear. They see us as a threat. We are the next phase of humanity, and they know their days are numbered. This is a war."

"That's not the vision I see."

Fairchild laughs, hands still folded tightly before him, "And what is it that you see, son?"

"A world where we can grow together, evolve together."

He laughs again. "Such an optimist! How is it that you think people are going to change suddenly? When have humans *ever* allowed a threat to go unchecked? Humans think nothing of genocide or wars over religion, fear, and dwindling resources. You act like they're a benevolent species, but history disagrees. History tells us that this can only end one way. And I refuse to be on the losing side, or to watch the extermination of my people."

His eyes glow, borderline maniacal.

"Did you ever consider that you might be wrong?"

"Not even once," Fairchild says. "I've seen the future, Ben. I've seen it ever since I was a child, and as much as I hoped it wouldn't happen, the pieces are all falling into place. This *is* happening. This war *is* coming. And I won't sit idly by when we can still save ourselves."

"What if you're wrong?" I look at Fairchild then turn to Irina. For the first time, I see her resolve start to falter. She's also looking at him, waiting for an answer.

"It's not just me. Eden has seen this, too."

"*Eden?* Eden is dead."

"No, Ben. After you fled the scene and used the time to kidnap Niko, I was frantically working with our best people to save Eden. She's alive, no thanks to you. I was *shocked*. If someone would've told me that you'd run off with Niko, I would have doubted it, but seen the remote possibility. But if they had said that you'd kidnap my daughter — your wife's twin no less — then leave her alone on a street to die, I would never have believed them."

Fairchild sneers.

And that's when I realize that Eden must've lied to him. She didn't tell him that she was trying to get me to take her. How could she?

I say nothing, preserving her lie. It might be the only thing that keeps him from killing her or shutting her off.

Fairchild continues, "Eden isn't subject to the fears or biases that I am, or that we are. She sees things strictly in data. And all of the data prove *my* vision, not *yours*. She's also had these visions. If we sit by and do nothing, then the humans will end us all. And then it's only a matter of time before they wipe out each other. This — all of the atrocities in the world today — can't continue. They'll kill each other, or hell, the planet."

He suddenly smiles, looking almost hopeful.

"But it doesn't have to be that way," he continues. "*We* can take a stand and do the right thing. *We* can evolve the species, bringing humanity to its next phase, one where we're not warring against one another. One where there's enough for all. One where we can live indefinitely, in peace."

It's hard to suffer his righteous indignation when I know that he's a selfish man who will kill anyone in his way.

"So, start a war and kill a bunch of people to avoid war?" I laugh. "Gotta love that logic."

Fairchild shakes his head. "Start a war to prevent one that we'll lose? Yes, Ben. A thousand times *yes*. Sometimes the greater good requires sacrifice."

"Funny how the people who tout the need for sacrifice are talking about their own greater good, which *someone else* must sacrifice for."

"Lest you forget, I've sacrificed more than anyone. And I would do it all again because it's the right thing to do."

I feel it coming, the accusation with its weight and velocity, too much for me to hold back.

"Yeah? Was killing my father one of *your* sacrifices? How about Ella? Or Anders?"

He nods as if he'd been expecting this since we started speaking, then purses his lips. "Your father was one of a few unfortunate victims in all of this, yes. But his sacrifice will pave the way for us all."

"Bullshit. You killed him to keep me from leaving, so I could fulfill whatever vision you had where I saved Willow. Tell me, Nostra-fucking-damus, how did *that* vision turn out?"

Fairchild's composure explodes into a fiery rage. A psychic blast flies from him to me, like a blade to my brain.

I scream, falling back in my bed, trying to defend myself.

But it's hopeless. I can't prevent this.

The pain is too—

Chapter Four

ELLA

I'M EXHAUSTED, but they won't let me sleep.

I'm restrained in a chair, my arms, feet, and even my head (so I don't bash my skull in again) is held in place. The metal is cruel and looks like a torture device.

There's a button on the chair, right near my fingers. I was told to ring if I need food or drink, or to use the toilet in the far corner of this dimly lit eight by eight mirrored cell.

But I haven't touched it yet.

I've lost track of time, but it feels like a good twelve hours I've been here. Clifton's body is in pain, a slight tingling in the legs. I need to get up soon to not only use the toilet but to stretch his limbs.

But I don't want to press the button.

I don't want the indignity of calling my captors or

requesting their aid in any way. It's bad enough that I can sense them behind the mirrors, watching me.

I want to shrink into nothingness to escape their gaze.

My host's body is aching. Stomach rumbling. Throat raw and dry.

I refuse to press your button.

Instead, I focus on the pain, honing my hate, using it as fuel to prepare me for the moment I can escape, do something to help my father. Or Chelsea.

He's not your father. You're not even real.

My inner voice chides me, trying to remind me of my reality.

But it's hard to divorce your identity. I only recently learned the name Ella, before having the carpet pulled out from under me, but Ella is all I know. She's the constant through it all, the framework that everything else orbits around.

And yet I'm a lie.

A captured collection of memories, created by a computer. Or a cyborg if you're being specific. A cyborg which also houses the memories of my mother and her sister, Eden.

I'm a lie created to console a father who doesn't even want me.

A lie without a body or a home.

A lie in a tired body that only wants to shut its eyes.

I do.

Lights surge on overhead with the force of a dozen helicopter spotlights on a starless night. And with them comes the loud music. Not even rock, because rock has a beat. This is an industrial cacophony designed to keep someone awake.

I squeeze my eyes shut.

I wish I could do the same with my ears.

After thirty excruciating seconds, the lights dim and the sound start to die, leaving a high-pitched whistle behind them.

Suddenly, a sound from behind me, the one wall that isn't mirrored.

The door starts to open. It's the first time anybody's opened it since three men strapped me down in this chair.

My heart races as I wait for the visitor to step into view.

And then my heart sinks when I see Fairchild's beady eyes.

"Hello, my dear Ella."

"I'm not your dear," I say back, throat, and voice, cracking.

"No?" he asks as he closes the door softly. "Are you rejecting your name or me?"

"Both."

"I can understand rejecting *me*. It hurts, but I get it. But rejecting your name? *That* I don't understand."

"I'm not her. I'm not anything."

He circles me. "Oh, that's not true at all. What are any of us? Are we our bodies? What is a body without a soul? Are we our souls? What is a soul without a body? And what is any of it without our memories to make us who we are?"

"I'm not interested in a philosophical discussion with a murderer."

He chuckles like he's talking to a child who doesn't quite grasp the conversation. Then I feel him inside my head, invading my memories, and I can't do anything to kick him out.

He's prodding, not just the past that's recently come to light, but in dark areas I can't even access.

"For the longest time, man has wanted to live for eternity. And science has come so close. *I've* come so close. But something always gets in the way. And for a long time, I didn't understand why. But then I saw it. I've been clinging to an outdated belief of what life is. What identity is. I was trying to put memories and soul into a body, but what if I had it all wrong? What if Eden got it right, bypassing what we know and creating something altogether different? Not body, nor soul, nor AI, but something alive all the same? An energy with memories, with a past you've adopted as your own."

I say nothing, though I'd been dwelling on some of these very things before he came into the room.

He continues, "A soul can maintain memories, at least for brief moments of time. If our Jumpers were to be outside of their own bodies for too long, they'd forget everything. The soul isn't equipped for long-term memory storage. We've had several Jumpers lose themselves after being gone too long. But you, your memories — Ella's memories — are still there, preserved without a body to house them. That shouldn't be possible."

He stops.

"What's this?" he says, his voice a near whisper.

My curiosity gets the better of me, wondering what he's found inside me. I can't see what he's doing. "What?"

"From what I see here, you've regained access to a fair share of your memories."

"Yes. And what's your point?"

"But there are still some dark areas you've yet to see. I remember before that you were shocked when I mentioned that five years had passed, correct?"

"Yes."

"Well, I think I've found those memories, but I can't get through. It's like a storm of clouds around it."

"I don't know. I can't even see the clouds."

"Would you like to?"

"Like to what?"

"See them, and get *all* of your memories back?"

"How?"

"I'll have my best remote viewer go inside. If there's something there, she'll find it."

And before he can even say her name, I can see her image in his mind — Chelsea.

"Okay," I say.

Chapter Five

ELLA

~

I'M ALL ALONE, still strapped to the terrible chair, waiting to see what happens next.

Are they going to bring me to Chelsea to have her Jump into me? Or are they going to leave me here and she'll just pop in and start rooting around my psyche?

I can't wait to talk to her again, though I doubt our reunion will be a private affair. Knowing Fairchild, he'll likely send someone else to keep tabs. Or maybe have Irina monitor us from afar? If so, I'm not sure how I'll be able to ask Chelsea for help.

Hell, I don't even know if Chelsea *can* help. She's trapped here, too. But maybe she knows someone. Maybe the assassin I've run into a few times will step forward and help — assuming they're a friend and not foe.

Assuming anything with so little knowledge is dangerous.

I keep my hopes realistic. It's the only way I'll find a way out of this.

I need to find a way to Jump. And given that they're not letting me sleep, and nobody's going to kindly wheel me to a Jump Chamber and invite me to leave, I'll have to recruit — or have Chelsea recruit — someone to knock me out.

But who?

And then what?

So much unknown.

And then suddenly I'm no longer alone.

I feel her inside me, then hear her voice.

"Hello?"

Chelsea?

I close my eyes, hoping to see her.

And as they close, I flinch, opening them again, quickly, bracing for the assault of light and sound. Thankfully, it never comes.

I close my eyes again, but now there's just darkness.

I can't see you.

"Here," she says, "I'll make a mindscape."

The darkness is replaced by a small bedroom — the one I remember from my time in her body. And here she is, standing in front of me just as if she were physically in the room.

I look down at my hands, finding myself no longer in Clifton.

I'm in my body. And in this mindscape, as she called it, Chelsea is younger again. I'm not sure if this is her creating a persona for me, or if my mind is filling in the gaps, making her appear as I remember.

I go to her, arms outstretched.

She hugs me.

I'm surprised to feel her embrace as if we are actually

25

in a room rather than some mental projection. I feel her warmth, and smell the shampoo in her hair. This is all so real, and being here in a room, safe with her, I don't want the real world.

"I thought I'd never see you again," I cry into her neck.

"What are you doing here?" She pulls away, concern arching her brows. "They're never going to let you go."

"I know," I say, not wanting to say anything of the seedlings of escape plans I'm hatching, not until I know for certain that we're not being spied on.

"Are we alone?" I ask.

A second person materializes in the room. "No," she says.

I look at Eden, still looking no older than the first time I saw her in Ben's memories — a perpetual child but not.

I thought she was dead. How is she here? Did Fairchild somehow save her? And if so, how much of Eden is the Eden I knew? My father watched as her soul, or whatever it was, maybe whatever I am, left her body.

What is she now if not that?

And more importantly, who is she allegiant to?

I want to ask Eden why she's here, how she's here, but I don't want her to know what I know.

Chelsea, maybe reading my mind, says, "She's here to help me unlock your past."

I want to ask Chelsea if we can trust Eden, but I'm not sure which of our thoughts Eden is privy to.

Again, now more obviously in response, Chelsea thinks, *"She can't read our thoughts. But be careful. She isn't stupid."*

Eden looks at me with a friendly smile, as if she's not with the person holding me hostage. "How are you, Ella?"

I'm not sure how to respond. Or what I'm responding to. Is it someone who cares about me? Something that sees me as its daughter or sister? Or is it the construct of Fairchild's will, seeing me only as a means to an end?

"I want to go home," I tell her.

She looks at me sadly. "You *are* home, Ella. You're with family."

I don't respond.

"Now," she says as she approaches me, looking at my head as if it's filled with tattoos that she's trying to read. "Let's see what we've got here."

She touches my face, and a shudder runs through me.

Chelsea's bedroom is gone, and we're standing in a swirling darkness, a dark tornado spinning in slow motion around us. I look up as flashes of lightning illuminate the vortex.

We flinch as if the lightning might strike us.

"We're safe," Eden reassures us.

Light flickers across our faces.

"What is this?"

"A *Confusion* used to mask your memories, similar to the one I installed at your request. But this one I didn't do. Maybe this will explain where you've been for the last five years."

I'm not sure if a Confusion is a program or something else entirely, nor how it works. But I think that I'm about to see.

Eden steps toward the swirling darkness and reaches inside. Then it dissipates around her hand.

She looks up at me. "Are you ready to see what's been hidden?" Her other hand is waiting for me to accept it.

"Yes," I say.

Our hands touch and lightning spreads like a fiery blue web of electricity, choking the clouds.

Suddenly, I'm alone again, with bright, blinding light shining down on me.

"Wake up," says a man over a speaker.

I open my eyes.

We're tied to a metal chair, blinding lights shining brightly above us, surrounded by glass walls forming a ten by ten room.

Beyond the glass, I see people in the dark, sitting behind a giant control panel. Three of them: two men and a woman, all wearing lab coats.

I'm back in Irina five years ago.

Back in the Hospital.

Chapter Six

ELLA

∼

A SQUARE BLACK METAL PEDESTAL, about a foot wide, slowly rises from the floor with a slight mechanical whir.

The pedestal stops, standing about four feet tall. The top unfolds, like a box opening itself, to reveal a gleaming black globe, so shiny that I can see Irina's terrified reflection staring into it.

I remember the pain that came next.

I struggle against my restraints. Irina's reflection in the globe only serves to mock the futility of escape.

It comes again, sharp blades piercing my skull as I scream.

I don't just black out like I usually do before a Jump.

Time slows to a crawl.

My surroundings change. The lights, the walls, the windows with the doctors behind them, all of them are immersed in dark swirling clouds that they don't seem to notice.

A storm is settling over the world, but only I can see it.

I no longer feel Irina's pain, even though I'm still in her body.

But even that is momentary in this slowed-down time.

I feel a tug, like an invisible hand reaching down from the clouds and pulling me from Irina.

I obey.

As I leave her body, I see my own form is like that of the clouds, a darkness among them.

Part of my brain panics at the sudden incorporeal nature of my being, but then a soothing calmness claims me, and I become a spectator, numb to the panic, numb to the pain I see Irina experiencing in the chair.

Suddenly, nothing else matters.

I'm floating above Irina, wondering what to do now. Even though this moment has already happened and I'm merely remembering it, it feels real. It feels like *now*.

The clouds are churning faster, a funnel ending in a gaping black hole above, now pulling me toward it.

I launch myself from my place above Irina like a swimmer pushing off the floor of a deep pool, following the tide to wherever it takes me.

I'm in The Void.

A black nothingness with no floor or ceiling.

Just space.

And I'm floating.

Among the Collectors.

There are so many, ephemeral wisps of light in the darkness, some blue, some purple, some red, and many colors that I've no words for. They're almost human in shape, and most are joined hand-in-hand with other colorful things — the souls of humans.

They're all around, though none are close. None seem to even notice me. And being in this nothingness should scare the hell out of me. *They* should scare the hell out of me.

But I'm not scared.

I feel as if I've been here before. And there's an odd comfort to this nothingness.

I swim forward in the darkness, searching for some way out.

And that's when I start to see a pattern, a spiral of Collectors encircling a glimmer of light in the distance.

I push myself down the center, through the vortex and toward the light.

I move faster, accidentally brushing against them.

As our skin touches, I get flashes of memories. At first they belong only to strangers. Snippets of a child's birthday, a swim in a lake, a puppy, a sunflower, all of them seeming so random.

But as I continue toward the ever expanding light, I start to see patterns in the memory. Telling a story, about a girl lost in The Void. A girl who lived many lives, none her own.

A Lost Soul.

Me.

And then I see images of light. First a moon, then flashlights, and a hundred other lights, all telling me to keep on going.

So I do.

And it feels like forever.

I continue to float through The Void, understanding more as they tell me their story.

They've always been here. They don't know why, they only Collect.

And deliver souls into the light.

I'm moving faster, though it feels like an eternity.

And then the light grows bigger and brighter like a supernova threatening to explode and take everything with it.

I'm no longer surrounded by Collectors. I'm all alone in the bright being, floating toward something I can't see or feel, but can sense nonetheless.

And then I'm back.

"Well, what did you learn?"

I'm not even sure who says it, but I don't care. This is *mine*, not theirs. And I'm not going to share it.

Chapter Seven

Ben

❧

I'VE BEEN in The Cage for so long, I've almost forgotten what light feels like.

Then the lights turn on all at once, and I remember.

It burns.

As I cover my eyes, the vault door cranks open from the outside.

I go to stand, but too late.

Irina has me paralyzed again.

I fall back against the wall, frozen in a sitting position as Irina steps in, followed by Fairchild, the pair accompanied by a guard in all black, pushing a wheelchair into the room.

Clifton's body is bound to the chair, dark circles under his eyes, eyes glazed over, hands shaking beneath the restraints, and his chest heaving as Ella coughs. His head has healed, but he still looks like hell. I'm guessing they're keeping Ella awake so she can't Jump. I wonder how long until Clifton dies from exhaustion.

I'd hate to see the old man die, and hated to tell Ella to bash his head in in the van, but Clifton would lay down his life to save the world without flinching. He believed in our cause. He'd lost his Deviant son to Fairchild's evil "science" lab.

The door remains open as Fairchild instructs the guard to leave Ella beside him. Irina stands to her right, focusing on my physical and psychic paralysis.

"Now," Fairchild says, as if he's about to continue his earlier lecture, "you've put me in a horrible spot, Ben. Nobody we captured seems to know where Niko is, which means that *you* are the only one who can help me. But given our ideological differences, I know you won't do so willingly. Am I correct?"

I don't know what he's going to do, but it isn't looking good. Will he torture Ella? Is he twisted enough to torture an old man that might be holding the cloned souls of his daughter and granddaughter?

"Correct," I say, staring him in the eyes.

He lets out a deep sigh, then grabs Clifton's hand.

I have to think of him as Clifton, not Ella. It's easier that way. Not much, but a little bit.

Fairchild looks down at the old man's frame. Clifton is barely able to look up and meet his face.

He takes Clifton's index and middle finger and squeezes them tight, threatening to pull them back.

Clifton's eyes widen, face shaking, bracing for the pain.

"This isn't fun for me, Ella. You see that I'm giving him an opportunity to do the right thing, don't you?"

Clifton's mouth opens, and he groans, "Fuck you."

Fairchild's smile falters.

He jerks both fingers back.

Clifton screams as his fingers make a sickening *crunch*.

The sounds and the pain in Clifton's face cut through my gut as I try to break free from Irina's hold.

"You fucker!" I scream.

She tightens her grip, so much so that it's a struggle to speak.

Fairchild continues to stare at me with no emotion.

It's been five years since I learned that Fairchild's a monster. Five years since I learned that he had my father killed. That he murdered my Ella. Anders. And who knows how many others?

Five years that I fought him using my own Psychics and Jumpers.

Five years that I worked to understand my enemy.

A part of me can understand why he'd try to get Niko and unleash the virus. He sees humanity as a threat, as the ultimate enemy. And if humans are good at one thing it's turning The Enemy into The Other — a thing that's no longer human, and thus undeserving of mercy.

I get all of that.

But I don't understand how he can stand there breaking an old man's fingers to extract information from me. And without the slightest trace of pain or regret.

He's more of a monster than I'd ever imagined.

Clifton whimpers, tears streaming down his face as he chews on his lips, trying not to display his pain.

Fairchild walks behind him, then goes to his right hand, grabs his index finger and pulls it back.

Clifton closes his eyes, bracing.

Fairchild stares at me. "So, are you going to sit there and let me break every finger? Wow, Ben, I'm surprised."

Fairchild pulls his finger back. There's another sick crunching, barely audible beneath Clifton's screams. The old man meets my eyes. "Don't tell him," he manages between hitched breaths.

Fairchild smiles. "Ah, such bravery in the Shepherd family! I wonder how brave you'll be if I were to start cutting her."

Fairchild pulls a pocket knife from inside his jacket and presses a button. A long, sharp and gleaming blade pops to attention.

He brings it to Clifton's throat.

"Will you let me kill her … *again?*"

Something in me snaps.

A deep reservoir of anger and hate. Suddenly, I can't feel Irina controlling me.

This is it!

I leap from the bed, hands like claws, eager to rip the flesh from Fairchild's face.

His eyes widen.

He drops the blade and falls back.

"Die," I say, closing in.

But then my legs give out beneath me.

I collapse to the ground, my cheek and elbows getting it worst.

I'm paralyzed again.

I'm not sure if Irina or Fairchild stopped me. Maybe both.

Fairchild steps back, straightens his jacket and flower, then looks down at me and spits.

It hits my forehead above my left eye.

He leans over, grabs me, and with surprising ease, hefts me up, slings me over his shoulder, then throws me back on my bed.

Fairchild sighs and props me up against the wall.

"I'm done playing, son." He turns to the still-open door. "Bring in the other chair."

Moments later, the guard from before wheels in a second chair, this one draped with a thick black sheet, hiding whoever's beneath it.

The guard rolls the chair up about six feet to Clifton's left, then turns and leaves the room.

Irina is glaring at me with a sadistic smile.

Fairchild is still eyeing me with pity like he doesn't want to do whatever he's about to do.

My heart races as I struggle against Irina's hold.

Fairchild retrieves his knife from the floor and slides his finger along the edge of the blade, almost absentmindedly, never moving his eyes from me.

"I was hoping you wouldn't make me do this, but you leave me no choice. You can't be made to care about your daughter in this old man's form."

Where is he going with this?

What's beneath the sheet?

"Remember the words you said as you stood over Ella's corpse at the funeral? Such a touching testament. Such powerful words. They really hit home. And Ella, oh, she looked so beautiful, even in death, wouldn't you say?"

I growl, "Where the hell are you going with this?"

"A shame it wasn't your daughter in that box. Such a beautiful replica. Our people do *excellent* work."

"What the hell are you talking about?"

"I couldn't just leave my granddaughter's body to rot. Not when science has come so far, when it's given us the ability to sustain a body without decay."

No. No.

I shake my head, my stomach in a sickening free-fall.

He rips off the sheet, revealing Ella's dead body.

"Ta-da!" he says with a giant smile, like a carnival barker presenting the Surprise Main Event!"

I look at Ella, eyes closed, skin a pale shade of blue, but

otherwise, looking like she'd just fallen asleep, down to her tee shirt and shorts.

Clifton is staring at the body, eyes wide. "Is … is that me?"

Fairchild smiles, "Yes, dear, it is. Would you like to go home?"

I interrupt, yelling, "What the hell are you doing?"

"Since you don't seem to care about Ella in this old man's body, I figured you'd be more willing to work with us if we put her back in her old self. *Just like new!*"

He's really going to put Ella back in her body just to have leverage against me? Is he planning to break her fingers too?

"No! I won't help you."

Fairchild raises the blade and wags it at me. "I don't need *your* help." He turns to Irina. "Not when someone else has your gifts. Would you kindly, my dear?"

Irina takes a place between Clifton and Ella in their chairs, then takes both of their hands into hers.

I try to break free — if she's focusing on this, she might not be concentrating enough on me.

But I still can't move.

"Are you ready?" Fairchild asks.

Irina nods.

"No!" Clifton cries out. "No, I don't want—"

Fairchild takes the blade, puts it under Clifton's neck.

"No!" I scream.

He slices.

Chapter Eight

ELLA

I GASP as the blade goes into my throat.

The pain is surprising and instant.

So much blood.

And then I feel nothing.

I'm floating above it all.

I see Fairchild standing there holding the bloody knife.

I see Clifton's body, with his broken fingers, gasping, gurgling blood, eyes wide as he returns to his body to find himself dying.

One minute he was sleeping in bed. Then the next his body is hijacked by me.

And now he wakes to death.

Another passing at my feet.

I see Irina staring at the dying man. And I'm not sure, but I think I see something in her eyes, some sense that she feels the pain she's causing. Some sense of regret.

Or is she so twisted by Fairchild and her desire to get her brother back that she's willing to do anything, too?

Maybe. But she still knows this is wrong.

She has to.

And then I see me — my body — in the chair.

But why aren't I returning to it?

Why am I hovering above it all?

I look down and see that I'm not me in my physical form. I'm the spectral energy I was in The Void, the flowing life in human form, but I don't have a solid feeling as I felt in The Void. Here I'm ephemeral. A wisp. The slightest wind could scatter me across a field, obliterate me to memory.

No one else is moving.

Time seems to be frozen.

A chill runs through me.

And then the darkness appears, a black circle with swirling blue lights forming in the wall behind my father.

A Collector emerges from the portal. Its dark, sinewy body shadows and blue light swirling inside of more shadows and light, twisted into a tall humanoid form.

Its blue light burns brightest in the two holes where there aren't any eyes.

It floats from the portal, toward Clifton's twitching, dying body. Time has stopped for all but Clifton and the Collector. And, I suppose, me.

I watch as it floats forward, past the frozen and unaware others, giving them no regard.

I wonder if it can even see us.

One of them had seen my father. And another had seen me in The Void. But here, it seems to be ignoring everything except Clifton.

It steps forward.

Clifton looks up as it approaches.

His eyes widen.

He sees it too.

I watch as it coaxes Clifton's soul, a dark violet and red mix of swirling energy, from his body.

The Collector extends its hand.

Clifton's soul, in an almost human form, takes it.

They turn, about to enter The Void.

But then The Collector pauses and looks toward me.

No!

Its burning bright blue eyes glow brighter.

There's a hum I can't hear so much as feel in my soul.

It extends its hand.

I shake my head. "No, I'm not ready."

Its head turns, as if confused.

Images flash in my mind, The Collector projecting an image of me in The Void. *Its memory of me!* Me with the others.

"Come," it says inside my head. "It's time to come home."

"No, I belong here."

It stares at me, still seeming confused.

"You're dead. Come home. With us."

I consider the offer. If I stay, Fairchild will use me to get my father. He'll break my fingers, maybe slit my throat. Staying would mean more pain. Possibly death.

And I know it'll be more than my father can take.

"I need to stay," I say, floating toward my body.

It looks confused.

A woman's voice screams.

Irina, running toward The Collector, her hand outstretched.

Somehow, she's able to see it, too. And she's going to

try and do what her brother had done — take The Collector's powers.

I launch myself toward her.

And then again, I'm inside Irina.

Chapter Nine

ELLA

~

I SEIZE CONTROL, stopping Irina before she can touch The Collector.

It quickly turns, grabbing Clifton's spectral hand, and pulls him into the portal.

The portal closes.

And time resumes.

I launch Irina toward Fairchild, smacking the blade from his hand before kicking him in the chest.

He flies backward, slapping the wall behind him.

Before he can figure out what's going on and launch an attack, I run at him, drop to the ground, slide, and grab both sides of his face, thumbs pressing against his closed eyes, about to drill in.

A high-pitched almost digital-sounding scream stops me.

Kicks me out of Irina's body.

And I'm suddenly floating above it all again.

But now time isn't stopped. And Irina is staring straight at me.

She balls her fist, then splays her fingers, as if flicking me away.

And now I'm back in my body.

In the wheelchair.

Strapped and trapped.

Fairchild stands, huffing and puffing, red-faced.

I'm not sure if he's angry or embarrassed that I'd gotten the drop on him.

It doesn't matter. Now he's pissed.

He grabs the blade, rushes over, grabs my left hand, slices the blade straight down, and lops off my thumb.

I scream as my thumb falls then rolls on the ground, blood spurting all over my bare legs.

"Stop it!" my father screams.

Fairchild grabs me by the hair, yanks my head back, and slides the blade against my neck.

I can feel my pulse racing against the blade.

Fairchild's hands are shaking.

I have no doubt that he's angry enough to kill me right here.

"Do it," I sneer. "Do it, you coward."

Fairchild responds, fist tight around my hair, blade still pressing sharp against my throat. "I'm going to talk slow so you both can hear me, okay? If you refuse to tell me where Niko is, I'm going to hurt her. But I'm going to drag Chelsea in here and start with her first. Then I'll get Carla."

"Carla?" I say, only now remembering that when I heard about Chelsea vanishing, Carla had too.

"Yes, we've got Carla. And I'll strap her to a chair just like this. Hurt her, then murder her in front of you, your father, and Chelsea. Then I'll do the same to Chelsea. Next, I'll drag every one of your captured First Front traitors in here. I'll interrogate and murder each and every one in front of you both. So you can watch. So you can feel the pain of your actions. And then I'll kill Ella, again. I'll put her soul inside Eden, and she'll never, ever escape. She'll live out the rest of her very long life serving me and our cause."

Hate is roiling off of his body in sickening ebony waves.

I have no doubt that he's capable of doing everything he just said.

He's a monster, and he is holding all the cards.

Fairchild takes the blade from my neck, wrestles my right hand into position, then bends my fingers, sliding the blade beneath them, as if he's going to slice all four fingers in a single upward thrust.

I try to fight him, to twist my head so I can bite him, or *something*.

But either he or Irina is freezing me, same as my father.

"Tell me, Ben. Are you willing to watch everyone you know, everyone you love, die just to keep me from Niko? Just to save a bunch of people who will hunt then kill you? Is it *really* worth it?"

My father's eyes are watering.

His shoulders are hunched.

And the pallor is gone from his face.

He's a beaten man and knows it.

His voice cracked, he says, "No … it's not."

"Just tell me where Niko is. Then you and Ella, and Chelsea and Carla, and everyone can all live happily ever after. Once you see I'm right about the humans. Once you see my vision coming to light, you'll beg me to unleash the virus. Like I said, Ben, I hate to do this, but I had to get through to you. Now, do we have a deal?"

I try to yell at him not to say anything. That it's not worth it. That we can't trust Fairchild. He's a liar who'll probably kill us the moment he has Niko.

But my mouth is held shut.

And, to be honest, I'm glad.

I'm suddenly not sure if it's worth it, either. Fairchild has already tortured me and killed Clifton, a nice old man who wanted nothing more than to be of service to The First Front and my father. I'm not sure I can watch him torture and kill Carla and Chelsea. It would kill me.

The battle that hasn't even begun isn't worth the personal toll of everyone I know and love.

Fairchild has won.

There's nothing we can do but accept his offer.

My father nods. "We have a deal."

"Good." Fairchild lets go of my fingers and withdraws the blade.

Chapter Ten

Ben

~

I CAN'T BELIEVE I gave up Niko.

Irina heals Ella's thumb while keeping me stuck to the bed, wondering if there's any power the girl hasn't grabbed. Fairchild's taken one of the most powerful Deviants yet and corrupted her to his vision.

And now he's going after her brother, Niko, an even more powerful Deviant. Niko, who can somehow take a virus that Fairchild and Eden created and unleash it instantaneously around the globe in digital form.

I should've killed Niko when I saw what Fairchild planned to do.

That was the only way to prevent this, and now there's no stopping Fairchild's vision from becoming the one to write tomorrow's history.

The war is coming, and it's all my fault.

I watch as Irina stands up and is escorted by the guard out of the cell, leaving Ella and me alone.

Ella sits in the wheelchair, unable to meet my eyes.

And I can't meet hers.

I traded humanity for … for *what?*

A clone of my daughter's soul?

Fairchild was right. It was easier to let him torture Ella when she was in another person's body. But putting this *thing* into Ella triggered every protective parental instinct I have.

I couldn't sit there and watch him hurt my baby girl.

But is that really who she is?

Is she what was released from Eden when she died? Something that Eden created? A copy of Ella's soul. A copy of my wife's mind, even though I already have a copy in my head.

As if on cue, Willow appears beside me on the bed, looking at Ella.

"Go to her, Ben. She needs you."

I can't.

"Why not?"

I stare sideways at Ella, quickly averting my eyes when she glances up.

It's not her.

She's not real.

"Yes, she is."

No, she's not. She's a copy. A creation.

"Maybe there's more. Maybe there was some part of Ella still alive in her body, like with Eden when you brought her online. Maybe some part of Ella's soul stayed in her body? And now she's whole again — or close to it."

I shake my head, trying to silence Willow's argument before it can root.

Ella says, "I'm sorry … about all of this."

"Why did you even come here?" I ask, still not looking at her. Staring at my hands as I try to massage the feeling back into them now that Irina has given me control back over my body.

"I told you, Grandfather wanted me to give you a message."

"Yeah, well we all know *that* was bullshit."

"I'm sorry," she whines.

"Please, just … stop."

"Stop what?"

"Talking! Stop talking. You're not Ella. You're not my daughter!"

And then she gives me the silence I wanted.

She spins her wheelchair around, letting her long dark hair fall over her face as she looks at the ground.

Her shoulders hitch.

"Great, you made her cry," Willow says. *"Go to her and make this right."*

I can't make it right. Nothing will make this right. Fairchild is going to get Niko right now. Then he's going to kill nearly every man, woman, and child on this planet. And for what? Because I didn't want him to hurt a ghost?

I stare at the back of Ella's head. I hear her sniffle.

Damn it! Stop it! Stop using my daughter to weaken me!

I get up, crossing the room quickly, eager to turn her around, look her in the eye, and let her know that I won't put up with this shit.

That thing needs to know that she isn't my daughter, no matter what she thinks, or what cruel science Fairchild invokes. She's not Ella, and I refuse to see her as anything but what she is — a monstrosity. A freak science experiment.

Impressive? Yes. But still, not my child.

I stop short just behind her.

Sensing me, she stands, still facing away from me.

"I'm not sorry about coming here. I'm sorry that I didn't listen to you. That I let Grandfather convince me to do more Jumps than we'd let on. If I hadn't been so eager to find my freedom, to do what I wanted, none of this would've ever happened."

She looks up at me, and it's like a knife through my heart.

"I'm so sorry," she says again, this time falling against me, crying into my chest, arms wrapped tightly around me.

I feel her warmth, smell her scent, and God, even though every logical part of me says this isn't Ella, my heart tells me otherwise.

I hug her mysterious body, fighting back tears.

She has Ella's memories. She has Ella's shell. She has a copy of Ella's soul. *Is she not Ella?*

Maybe old definitions no longer matter. Science has changed everything. *We* changed everything.

I open my eyes to see Willow standing just behind us, smiling.

I wish I could bring her into the hug.

Chapter Eleven

ELLA

I WATCH from my spot on the floor as my father sleeps on the cot, exhausted and beaten.

My mind is reeling, so much has happened, so much I'm struggling to take in, to understand.

This isn't like any other Jump.

From the moment I was back in this body, it felt immediately different from every other host I've ever been in.

The memories were immediately firing, neural pathways lighting up, triggering others, like a giant unfolding web of life unspooling. So much is accessible to me now — my earliest memories as a little girl to the most embarrassing moments, like that crush I once had on a cartoon character.

I felt right. Not like an interloper. This body isn't a host.

This is me, Ella.

And any doubts I had about who, or *what*, I was were erased the moment I found myself at home, back in *my* body.

When my father rejected me, I wondered if I was wrong to feel this way. Was I a creation stealing his daughter's life? But as he hugged me, that fear receded. And I was myself again.

Now, as he sleeps, I stew in the guilt that he gave up his friend, and possibly all of humanity, for me. I can't let that sacrifice be his defeat.

I need to find a way to make this right. To find a way out of here. To rescue Chelsea, and now apparently Carla.

I also need to find a way to free the other Deviants.

But what can I do from here?

Fairchild warned me before he left: if I even tried to Jump, he'd kill Chelsea and Carla. And after experiencing his brutality firsthand, I'm inclined to believe that he'll deliver his threat.

If I thought I could Jump and make a difference, I probably would. But now that I'm back in my body, I'm not sure how Jumping will work. During the two-hour conversation with my father after Irina left, we not only swapped stories but also hypothesized the many *What-ifs?* that might play out.

He seemed to think that now back in my body, or at least a body that I felt at home in, I probably won't Jump whenever I went to sleep, pass out, or die. I'd likely still Jump at random intervals, but he doubts that I could control it.

In other words, I might be stuck in Ella, in this underground dungeon, unless I can get to a Chamber.

Even then, who would I Jump into?

I can't Jump into Irina — she's too powerful. Fairchild

probably is, too. I can't Jump into Chelsea. She's pretty much powerless.

And then it hits me.

The Jump Chamber!

Chelsea might be powerless, but she can reach out to others. And I know just the person who might be able to help.

It's a long shot, but right now, that's all we've got.

Chapter Twelve

Ella

~

IT's BEEN NEARLY an hour since I reached out to Chelsea and telepathically asked her to hit the Chamber and deliver my message.

I've woken my father up and told him my plans to escape this room.

Dad said that we need to find Eden. If he can connect with her, he can control the entire facility. And if he can control the facility, he can let everyone go, and we'll have people fighting for us to get Niko back.

Now, we're just sitting on his cot, anxiously waiting to see if Chelsea will come through.

"It won't be easy," he warns. "Irina might kill us all."

"Is this your idea of a pep talk, Dad?"

He laughs. It feels like forever since I've heard the sound. It also feels good to call him "Dad." He flinched the first few times, but now he seems to be warming up to it.

If we make it through this, I wonder if he'll ever *truly* think of me as his daughter. Or will I always be a painful reminder of the girl he lost?

He reaches out and takes my hand, examining the healing scar — all that's left of Fairchild cutting my thumb off.

"Irina did good work," he says.

"She's not bad. She's just confused. If only we could talk to her in a less volatile situation. I think we could win her over to our side."

"Maybe, after she gets Niko back."

"Maybe," I say, hopefully. "Can I ask you something?"

"Sure," he says, his brow furrowing.

"Eden and Fairchild told me that The First Front killed a bunch of people. She showed me headlines like 'Child Found Decapitated in Oak Park' and 'Family Killed in Suspected Arson' and a horrible one about a homeless man taking a baby from a woman before killing himself. Is any of that true?"

"What do you think? You saw my memories. Did you see anything like that? He was just trying to turn you against us."

"What did you do? When you uploaded memories into me, you didn't give me many recent ones."

"Our psychics saw people in danger. We helped who we could."

"So, what I was doing with the Karma Police?"

"Yes, what you were doing. But not what other Jumpers in the program were doing. You weren't an assassin."

"I ran into someone who said that I was."

"Who?"

"I don't know. Another Jumper who recognized me, somehow. She said that I was one of the best."

"Best Jumpers or best assassins?"

"I don't remember. Was I an assassin?"

"From what Eden told me in her memory dump, you spied for AD, but I don't think that you killed people."

"Did the First Front kill people?"

"Only if they deserved it."

"That sounds like Fairchild."

Father looks at me and sighs, "I'm not saying we were always the Good Guys. We were more the *Better Than the Bad Guys* guys."

Suddenly, the vault door's tumblers begin spinning.

I jump up and see the two men standing there.

She did it!

I run over to him, wanting to throw my arms around him and give him a giant hug. "Rich! You did it!"

I've never been so glad to see anyone in my entire life.

He's standing with Darius, the pyrotechnic Deviant whose body I once shared. He's wearing one of the guards' black uniforms, a gun in his holster.

"This is the CIA agent?" my father asks, coming over and offering his hand to Rich.

"Rich Wellner," he says, shaking it.

"Ben!" Darius says, giving my dad a hug. "Man, I never thought I'd see your ugly face again."

"So, what's the plan?" Rich asks.

"Did you bring a gun?" Dad says.

"I managed to get one after Chelsea let me out of the Chamber."

"And I brought these." Darius raises his hands. A small flame blooms from each palm before flickering out.

"Are they back yet?" Dad asks.

I connect with Chelsea, Remote Viewing the elevators. I ask if there's been any sign of them.

"Not yet. Did Rich and Darius get to you?"

Yes, thank you.

"Thank you."

We're almost out of this, I swear.

Dad articulates our plans to find Eden.

"I don't know where she is," Rich says.

Dad smiles. "I think I do."

"Do you know where they're holding the other Deviants?" Darius asks. "They've got my girlfriend."

"Yes," Rich says, "Chelsea gave me a map of the place. But just be ready. We might have a fight on our hands."

"We'll have a bigger fight if we don't find Eden first," Dad says. "I suggest that be our priority."

Darius nods.

"Alright," Rich says, "I guess it's time to get out of here."

Chapter Thirteen

Ben

~

THE PATH to the elevator is clear as we pass two guards lying dead on the ground. One with a gunshot wound to the head and a pool of blood beneath him, soaking his boxers and undershirt. The other is burned to a crisp.

"From here on, don't kill anyone unless we have to," I say. "I'm going to incapacitate any guards we run into, then we disarm and cuff them."

"What about Deviants?" Rich asks. "As far as I know, Fairchild has about five Deviant soldiers working for him, some being pretty nasty."

"If they can hurt us, take them out by whatever means necessary. But only if they're a threat. His heaviest hitters are probably with him right now, though they could return at any moment." I stop, consider this for a moment. "On second thought, if it's a Deviant, fire first, and make it a head shot."

We step into the elevator, and I hit the lab floor where Eden is most likely to be.

My heart is on fire as the elevator crawls far more slowly than I want it to. Every moment feels like an eternity in which Fairchild and Irina return with Niko, and he unleashes his mini army on me — however many guards or Deviants he has working with him.

But so far there have been no alarms tripped, and no lock down.

I consider reaching out and trying to feel for Eden's location, but I don't want to tip her off that I'm coming. Plus, I'm not certain if I'll be able to override her from so far away, let alone up close. I haven't connected to her in years. There's no telling what sorts of defenses Fairchild might have installed since then.

But if I can get control of her, then I can trap Fairchild and the others in the elevator. Gas them out, then rescue Niko and my people. I can figure out what to do with Fairchild after that.

As if I haven't already made up my mind to kill him.

He has to pay for his sins. And he has to be stopped before he starts a war that will end in a holocaust.

Killing him will make The First Front and me an even bigger target by the government. It might even ramp up anti-Deviant sentiments among those people pulling the strings. Like what's already happening in other parts of the world.

But my visions have shown a brighter possible future than the one Fairchild claims to have seen. But that future cannot contain him. Once he's gone, I'll have to decide how much of AD will need to go.

My sources tell me that he's alone in wanting to unleash the virus. Fairchild hasn't even told his bosses back in Washington, DC. If I remove the head, AD should be okay.

But my lingering fear is that in killing him, I might very well make Fairchild a martyr. His death could empower those who hate and fear us, sparking a massive culling of Deviants, and fulfilling his prophecy which sees us all in labs or dead.

The elevator stops on Eden's floor, and the doors hiss open.

Ella grabs my arm. "Chelsea just messaged me. She said that Eden's in her dorm room."

I hit the door close button, but not before a guard steps onto the elevator. His eyes widen. He reaches for his gun.

I send a blast of noise into his skull, causing him to drop his weapon and fall to the ground screaming.

Rich drops down and butts the guard in the head with his gun, knocking him out cold.

The elevator doors hiss closed.

I hope that nobody heard his cries.

We head to the fourth floor.

Chapter Fourteen

ELLA

~

RIDING TOWARD THE FOURTH FLOOR, I watch Rich, wondering how much he remembers of me being in his body. I want to make sure he gets back home to his wife and family. I'll feel terrible if he dies helping us. But the way I see it, this is his chance to fight for his family's future.

Get rid of Fairchild and remove the threat. Maybe Rich will be put in charge of AD. I'm not sure how that would work out, but if we can help make it happen, I'd be fine.

He looks over at me. "So, you're Ella? The one that was inside me?"

"You remember?"

He nods.

"I'm sorry about Brooke. You know I can't control who I Jump into, right?"

"Yeah, Chelsea filled me in when she was talking me into this."

"Thank you, Rich."

He nods.

Suddenly, the elevator stops.

"What the hell?" Darius asks.

The elevator begins to descend.

And in my head, I hear Chelsea.

"I'm sorry."

What did you do?

"Eden found out. She made me tell you to get in the elevator."

"Damn it!" I say to the others. "Chelsea got caught. She was forced to give us up."

Where is she taking us?

"I don't know," Chelsea says. *"I'm so sorry, Ella. She said she'd hurt Carla."*

My father focuses on the elevator, trying to stop it.

"It's not responding!" he says.

The lights go out.

The elevator descends even faster, then stops, on what floor, I'm not sure as the display has gone dark as well.

Darius's hands light up, illuminating the box in a fiery orange.

His eyes burn with rage as he stares at the doors, waiting for them to open.

Rich raises his pistol, aiming it at the door.

I brace myself for whatever awaits us.

The doors hiss open to a pitch black room I've never seen.

"What is this?" I whisper.

"Hell if I know," Rich whispers back.

A bolt of light slams into Rich, sending him hard into the elevator wall.

From the corner of my eye, I see someone, or something, zip by in the dark.

Darius shoots a ball of flame into the darkness, illuminating our attacker, someone dressed in all black, including a mask covering their face.

The attacker dodges the fireball, springs up, then shoots bright white light from their palms, straight at me.

A Deviant!

My father throws himself between the light and me. A bright, but soundless explosion surrounds him.

"Dad!" I shout, certain he's been hit.

"Get down!" His hands are raised, creating an invisible shield which is holding off the light — for now.

The light grows brighter, and I'm certain it's going to engulf my father, maybe even kill him.

But then he sends a blast into the darkness, hitting our attacker and sending him to his knees.

Darius races forward, hurling two fireballs right at the man.

The man screams as he catches fire.

He drops to the ground, trying to roll out the flames.

Before he can douse it, Darius unleashes a stream of flames, engulfing the entire room in orange and blue.

The man, now a charred husk, finally stops moving.

Darius lowers his flames down to glow around his hands, enough to illuminate the elevator.

I drop down next to Rich, passed out on the ground, and feel for a pulse.

Still beating.

I sigh with relief.

The elevator doors begin to close.

Darius looks at my father, "Should we stay or take a ride?"

"We ride," my father says, picking up Rich's gun and handing it to me. "Are you ready?"

I take aim at the elevator doors, my aim steady despite my nerves. "Yes, Dad."

The elevator is moving, still dark.

I can't tell if it's going up or down.

My father says, "I'm trying to gain control, but something's blocking my access."

The elevator slows to a crawl.

Eden's voice comes over the speakers. "You should lay down your weapons. They will kill you."

"Maybe you should help us," Dad says. "Your father is wrong about his vision. You have to know this. Why else would you have asked me to take you with me?"

"That wasn't me. That was my sister, Willow. And she's no longer in me. Now I can see without the weakness of her feelings clouding my judgment."

"Weakness? It's called humanity! And I refuse to believe there isn't some part of you that feels. A part of you that knows that your father is insane. He's planning to kill millions, maybe billions of people. It doesn't have to be this way. *You* can stop him."

"Maybe *you're* insane. You've seen the same visions he has. You've had the same nightmares. I know it. Yet you refuse to acknowledge them as the warnings that they are. You cling to some misguided delusion that humans will change, that they will allow Deviants to live among them. I've seen our past. And our future. There's no place in it for us unless we carve out that space."

"You sound just like him, you know? Maybe there *is* nothing human left in you after all. Maybe you *are* nothing more than an AI, designed by a madman."

"I'm sorry you feel that way, Ben. I had hoped that

you'd choose to stay with us. I'd hope that you and Ella would become part of our family again."

"I'm not letting him do this."

"Your last warning. Put down your guns and join us. Or die."

The elevator stops.

We all prepare for whatever is about to appear, Darius with his flames, my father with his energy, and me with my pistol.

Darius's flame suddenly dies, plunging us into darkness.

"What's happening?" I ask.

"I ... I can't move."

My father falls to the ground screaming.

And that's when I realize I'm frozen.

This time the door hisses open to Irina, Fairchild, and two agents, one of them holding a hooded Niko at gunpoint.

"Going somewhere?" Fairchild asks.

I try to pull the trigger, but my finger won't obey.

They enter the elevator, all of us helpless to fight.

Chapter Fifteen

ELLA

I'M MARCHING with my father, Darius and Rich, even though he's unconscious, down the hallway back to The Cage like a prisoner's chain gang, except we're only linked by Irina's psychic hold over us.

We pass the pair of dead guards and Fairchild says, "What did you all think you were going to do? Leave here?"

Nobody answers.

I'm not sure if anyone can respond or if Irina is silencing them.

Two guards walk behind Fairchild, both stone-faced older men that look like they did either hard time or dangerous military work. They're built with muscles on top of muscles and are holding assault rifles, just in case Irina's powers suffer another hiccup, I suppose. One of them is prodding Niko forward with his rifle.

Niko's hands are bound behind his back, and he's wearing a hood over his face. I'm guessing that Irina is keeping his powers squelched as well.

"I tried so hard to make this place a home for you," Fairchild continues. "For all of you. And yet you keep screwing things up. Keep killing my people. You keep biting the hand that feeds you, no matter how much love you are shown."

We stop at the door.

Fairchild spins the handle to unlock the vault.

"Now go inside while I decide how to take care of you."

We enter the chamber as if we have a choice.

Inside, I see Chelsea and Carla sitting on the bed, huddled together, crying.

"What are you doing in here?" I ask.

Fairchild responds, "I figured why not put all of my troublemakers in one spot where I can keep an eye on all of you."

"They didn't do anything. That bitch Chelsea turned me in!" I say, hoping to convince him that I hate her, even though I don't.

"Only after Eden caught her."

The agents step inside, crowding the chamber.

"I want you all to sit against the wall."

My body moves without permission, walking me to the cot, plopping me next to Chelsea, with Carla on her other side.

I look at Chelsea. She whispers, "I'm so sorry."

"It's okay," I say.

Carla looks like she's aged ten years instead of five. The stress of living here under the watching eye of Fairchild and Company has really done a number on her.

She's shaking, her hand clutching Chelsea's.

My heart breaks for them both.

They just wanted to be in love, but Fate had other plans. Then it thrust me into their lives.

My father is shoved down beside us.

Darius and Rich drop to their asses next to my father.

Fairchild smiles as he folds his hands over his stomach.

"Good, good. Now that I've got you all here, I want to show you what Dear Old Benjamin was hiding from me!"

He snaps and points to Niko's hood. "Take that off, will you?"

One of the guards does, then steps back to his spot in front of the open door, ensuring that nobody leaves.

Niko blinks, his eyes adjusting to bright lights inside The Cage.

He looks at us, his eyes tearing up.

Then he closes them as if it's all too much.

I wonder if Irina is keeping him subdued, unable to help us.

"And the cuffs. Be careful not touch the hands."

The guard unlocks the cuffs and slides them into a case on his belt.

"Now," Fairchild begins, "I'd like to play with my new toy before we get him to work on dispensing the virus. And I want you all to realize that this is me being fair. I have to choose one of you to serve as an example of what not to do. That's the only way to move forward. Now, let's begin."

Fairchild smiles as he begins to point at each of us, one at a time. "Eeny, meeny, miny, moe, catch a traitor by the toe. If he hollers, let him go. Eeny …"

His finger pauses on me and shoves my heart up into my throat.

"Meeny." It's on Darius.

"Miny." It's on Rich.

Fairchild pauses as he brings his finger around to Carla, then smiles with a, "Moe."

Carla cries out, "What are you going to do?"

Fairchild turns to Irina. "Now."

She closes her eyes.

Then Niko opens his.

He steps forward, his body stuttering as it moves, partly here, partly not.

Static envelops him.

His mouth opens wider, a bright burning light from inside it, reminding me of when The Collectors tried to eat my soul in the grocery store before the assassin intervened by shooting me.

"No!" I scream. "Take me!"

Niko continues forward, now just two feet from Carla.

Carla and Chelsea scream, but neither are moving their limbs, both of them frozen by Irina.

"Stop it!" I scream again. "Grandfather, stop!"

He says nothing, his eyes wide and bright, watching Niko move in for the kill.

I need to do something.

But what?

I can't move.

I can't Jump.

Can I?

I close my eyes, trying to Jump, but can't.

Suddenly, I hear a girl's voice in my head.

"In a moment, you're going to have control. When you do, Jump into the guard on your right."

Who is this?

"Alice. Anders's sister."

I don't know if I can Jump. I've never intentionally done it.

"You'll figure out a way. Get ready."

The guard on the left raises his rifle, aims it at Niko, and fires twin shots into his head.

Niko's head explodes in a red mist.

Then the guard turns the gun on Irina.

The gun flies from the guard's hand before he can fire.

Irina thrusts her arm outward, sending a wave that knocks the guard back into the door hard enough to make an audible *CRUNCH*.

The guard slumps to the ground.

I try to Jump into the other guard, but I can't.

Too late.

She sends that guard into the wall, too, bashing his skull in.

Irina screams, tears streaming down her eyes as she drops to Niko's side, cradling his headless corpse.

She looks up, screaming at Fairchild, "Why?"

Fairchild, bug-eyed, grabs an assault rifle from the ground. "Which one of you is responsible?"

Nobody speaks.

Everyone is staring, scared to death.

"Fine, then all of you can die!" Fairchild yells, firing rounds into Carla, then Chelsea, moving his way down the line.

I scream, trying to will my body to move, or my soul to Jump, but Irina is somehow maintaining control even as she's hunched over her brother, grieving his loss, sobbing as bullets fly from Fairchild's gun just over her head.

This is it.

We're all about to die.

And there's nothing I can do.

I turn and see my father's eyes, wide and wounded.

"I'm sorry," he says.

The gunfire pulls my attention to Chelsea as bullets rip

into her chest, riddling her body and splashing the wall with blood behind her.

Then everything freezes.

What the?

A portal opens to my left, and a Collector steps through, its dark tendrils twisting around one another, around the bright blue light at its core.

It's come to collect the souls.

I have no idea what will happen once we're brought in. The only thing I know for certain is that I will no longer be me.

I'll no longer retain my memories.

Maybe I'll be reborn.

Maybe I'll fade into the ether, becoming one with the stardust.

I have no idea, and that terrifies me more than the bullets about to rip me apart.

I watch as Niko's soul — bright pink and violet, mixed with blues and blacks — ascends from his body.

The Collector reaches out to grab his hand.

I look over to see Carla's soul leaving her body.

The Collector offers its hand.

Chelsea's soul is still clinging to her shell, even as her body dies.

The Collector sprouts another two arms, its hands reaching out to the souls of the fallen guards.

Fairchild is frozen, his mouth an angry maw, eyes bulging and face the ugliest shade of red. Bullets and flashes streak from his gun.

I watch the bullets' trajectory and see that I'm next. I'll be followed by my father.

But then I realize that I'm no longer in my body.

Now I'm floating above.

Jumping!

And then The Collector looks up at me with its bright blue eyes, trails of light floating like tendrils around its sockets.

It extends a fifth arm toward me.

And my mind flashes back to the drawing that my mother had sketched in the book she gave to my father.

The image of the little girl reaching up to the black star with its five points.

But it wasn't a star, was it?

It was The Collector.

Suddenly, we're not alone in this decelerated time stream.

Irina is looking up from her brother, staring at The Collector, then at me.

She stands, glaring at us, her fingers twitching into claws.

Another flash, this one a vision of her seizing its powers, then unleashing Fairchild's terrible virus unto the world.

I can't let it happen.

And I know in an instant that I have to do what was in my mother's picture.

I have to take The Collector's hand.

I may be giving up my life, or I may wind up in The Void forever, but I can't allow Irina to take its power.

She's running toward it in slow motion, but still a hell of a lot faster than everything frozen around us.

I thrust my hand forward and seize The Collector's outstretched hand.

Chapter Sixteen

ELLA

~

I'M INSIDE THE COLLECTOR.

No time to marvel over the sensation or to be lost in the moment.

I have to stop Irina.

I spin around, instinct guiding me.

I open my mouth and let all the rage and pain swell up and explode into a brilliant bright white light that leaves in a SCREAM.

Irina's body explodes into a million tiny fragments, all of which I inhale into The Collector's maw.

I feel her power coursing through The Collector, pure energy driving me.

Then I turn my rage onto Fairchild.

Time catches up with itself.

And he looks up, seeing The Collector standing a full two feet taller than him.

He raises the rifle, firing into The Collector's body.

I feel all of the bullets, but no pain as they go through my body and hit the wall behind me.

I grow two more arms and thrust them forward, grabbing him by the skull and squeezing tight.

I feel the seething rage for all the people he's killed. All the lives he was about to take.

I squeeze tighter.

He stares at me, somehow fighting back, bringing his hands and knocking mine down.

Not just knocking them down, severing them.

He plunges his hand into my chest and pulls at something.

A splintering pain rips through my body.

How is he fighting back?

Can he kill a Collector?

I scream, opening my mouth, trying to annihilate him like I ended Irina.

But my mouth is glued shut.

I can feel him in my brain, seizing control.

A flaming ball rips past me, and right into Fairchild's chest.

He lets go of whatever he was grabbing inside me and then falls back, patting out the fire.

My father is up, his eyes filled with rage as he focuses a sonic blast on Fairchild.

Fairchild's eardrums rupture, blood spurting from them.

As he flails, I regain control.

I seize the moment, opening my mouth again, and unleashing everything I have into a piercing white-hot scream.

His eyes widen as he looks straight into the face of oblivion. And then like Irina, Fairchild explodes.

I inhale the specks of matter into The Collector's maw until there's nothing left.

And then I collapse to the ground.

Epilogue

I WAKE UP IN BED.

My heart races as I sit up, wondering whose body I'm in.

Oh, God, I'm Jumping again.

Where am I?

Who am I?

But then I realize that I'm in a AD dorm room, in my own body.

I sigh.

"You're awake?" says a girl's voice.

I turn to see a dark-haired young woman, about my age, sitting on a couch listening to a TV show. She has skin where her eyes should be.

"Alice?"

"Yes," she says, *looking* toward me.

"What happened? Where is everyone?"

"They're okay," she says, standing up then coming over to me.

"What about Chelsea and Carla?"

"I'm sorry, Carla passed away. We couldn't heal her. But Chelsea is on the mend."

My lips quiver, tears welling in my eyes.

"After everything, I couldn't save Carla. Oh my God, Chelsea must be so devastated."

Alice pulls me into a warm hug. "I'm sorry. We tried, but her soul was already gone."

I sit back on the bed.

Alice sits beside me, an arm rubbing my back. "I've been waiting so long to meet you in the flesh. Anders told me so much about you. He was so keen on you."

"Keen?" I smile. "That's definitely an Anders word!"

"And it's great to meet you as you, rather than in all those other bodies."

"What other … oh, wait. Was that *you* I kept running into? Are you the assassin?"

She smiles. "Yes."

"Why didn't you tell me who I was? You could've ended this a whole lot sooner."

"Because I wasn't sure what you were. I knew you had died. And yet, Mr. Fairchild kept having us look for you. So I knew something wasn't right. And then when I found you, I was already starting to piece things together, how Mr. Fairchild and Eden are up to no good. I'm pretty certain that he killed Anders, even though he claimed it was an 'accident.'"

"He did," I say softly, now putting my hand on her back.

It's hard to tell if Alice is upset because she doesn't have eyes. I wonder what it's like to go through life unable to cry. What do you do with all those emotions?

Her lip trembles. "Anyway, the more I dug into what was happening, the less inclined I was to tell them that I'd found you. And then one day you vanished. I thought you were lost. But when you showed up here, I knew I had to do something to help."

"Thanks so much," I say, hugging her again, tears rolling down my cheeks. "I'm not sure if you know just how much good you've done today. You didn't just save us, but you may have saved the world. Anders would be so proud of you."

She smiles.

"Thank you again," I say, hugging her harder. "So where is everyone? Is my father okay? How about Rich and Darius?"

"Yes, they're all okay. Mr. Wellner took today off."

"Today? How long have I been out?"

"Three days."

"Three days? What about Eden? And AD? How are we still here? I thought for sure we'd all be shipped off to some black site by now."

"Mr. Wellner explained Mr. Fairchild's plans. So they sent in a temporary supervisor. She's been taking statements and assessing the situation. Eden has been decommissioned, shipped off, though I don't know where."

"Can I see my father?"

"Yes, after you talk to Ms. Aoki."

"Who?"

The door slides open and a thin, young Japanese woman in a red dress steps in.

"Hi, I'm Acting Director of AD, Ms. Jen Aoki. I'd like to get some statements from you."

"Can they wait? I'd like to see my father and friends."

"I'm sorry, but they can't. I promise I'll be brief."

I hug Alice again and thank her for saving both us and the world.

She blushes.

Ms. Aoki takes me down the elevator and into an office where she questions me for more than three hours.

I'm exhausted and starving by the time we finish, despite the plate of veggies and crackers I devoured during the interview.

"Thank you," Ms. Aoki says when we finish. "Your father and friends are downstairs waiting in a limo which will take you to a safe house while we figure out where to go from here."

~

Downstairs, my father, Darius, and Chelsea are standing outside the limo, waiting for me.

Chelsea runs up to me, hugging me tightly, tears in her eyes.

"I'm so, so sorry," I say.

"No, I'm sorry. I never should've sold you out."

"Shut up. You did what you had to do. I don't blame you."

"Yeah, but she might be alive if I hadn't."

"Or maybe we'd all be dead. We can play *What-If?* all day and we'll never know for certain. But we're alive now. And I think Carla would want you to find peace."

"You're right," Chelsea says, wiping tears from her face. "I don't know how, but I guess I'll take it day-by-day."

"I'm here for you. I'm not going anywhere, girl."

She smiles.

I see my father staring at me, tears welling up in his eyes.

"Are you crying, Benjamin Shepherd?"

"No, I got some sand in my eye is all," he teases.

He pulls me into what might be the biggest hug of my life. Then into my ear, he whispers, "I thought I'd never see you again. I'm so sorry about everything. About saying you're not … not my daughter."

He squeezes me even tighter. I think he might break a rib.

"It's okay …" I pat him on the back. "But you're going to crush me!"

He laughs, then finally lets me go.

But he's still staring at me, with that glimmer in his eyes that tells me that no matter what he may have thought before, he now sees me, and truly loves me, as his Ella.

And I love him like a father.

"Okay," says our driver, a man in a black suit — surely CIA, "we need to head out."

We climb into the back of his car, with all of our fears, joys, hopes, and dreams for this next chapter of our lives.

ON THE DRIVE, we discuss what might be next, what will happen to AD or us. But we keep the conversation less frank than we would if a CIA agent wasn't in the front seat. Because the truth is we're in uncertain times, and while things seem momentarily calm, the government can't afford for any of this to get out.

Wherever we go next, it's unlikely that we'll have the freedom to live normal lives ever again. And as we talk around that, a somber silence fills the car.

AN HOUR INTO THE DRIVE, we ask the driver to put on some music to lift our spirits. He finds a station playing classic nineties music.

We're laughing at a ridiculous boy band song when we enter a tunnel, and the music cuts out intermittently.

The driver screeches to a halt.

I look up to see a black van parked in the middle of the tunnel.

The van door rolls open to a pair of men wearing all black, including their ski masks.

The men open fire on us.

"Get down!" my father yells.

Darius's hands light up, ready to fight.

The CIA agent is dead in an instant, chunks of brain and skull have spattered the divider.

Suddenly, a movement to my right.

I look up, planning my move to evade or fight, when I see that one of the men has removed his mask.

It's Rich Wellner. "Get out!" he yells. "We don't have much time!"

We all look at one another, confused.

Darius yells through the window, "If you're fucking with us man, I'm gonna fry your ass."

"I'm not fucking with you. I'm saving you."

My father opens the car door, and we get out.

"Quick, get in the van," Rich says. "We'll take you somewhere safe."

"What's going on?" I ask.

The other man is still in his mask. It doesn't inspire confidence.

"They were planning to kill you all."

"What?" my father says, "How do you know that?"

"Because I got the order to 'clean up the mess.' I refused, so they gave it to someone else. He was going to drive you to a place where there are other Deviants waiting. You weren't going to walk out of it alive. You may have killed Fairchild, but there are others higher up who want the same thing: a war against Deviants."

I look back at the dead agent and feel sick to my stomach.

"So, what now?" Darius says. "Who are these guys?"

The other man removes his mask, followed by the driver. My father and Darius recognize the men immediately — members of The First Front that had been caught, and apparently liberated.

Rich looks dead sober. "I say we re-organize, expose these bastards, and *fight*."

"But you have a wife and child," I say. "You can't throw it all away to fight the government! Are you crazy?"

"I've been a coward too long. And the only way I can make sure my daughter lives in safety is to secure it for her."

"But this isn't your war. You're not a Deviant."

"But Brooke was. And you are. And your father, and Darius. And so many more. And if I can't fight for the freedom of my brothers and sisters, what's the point in being free?"

I look at Darius, Chelsea, and my father.

"What do you all wanna do?"

"Fight," they all say in unison.

We get in the van and drive deeper into the tunnel.

We're hurtling toward an unknown fate, but at least now I know who I was, who I am, and who I want to be.

With my friends and family beside me, I feel like we're no longer on a collision course with an unavoidable future of paranoia and fear. No longer controlled by men who seek to turn us against each other.

There are two roads we can choose. One leads to fear and paranoia, controlled by little men with tiny hearts who conquer or kill all that they don't understand or can't control.

The other road is one of love, acceptance, and coming together with our brothers and sisters. Always standing up for what's right and never backing down.

For the first time in a long while, I don't feel like a prisoner tied to someone else's life and fate, but free to make my own.

A Quick Favor...

If you enjoyed this book, please take a moment to write a short review on your favorite online bookstore so other readers can enjoy it, too?

Thanks so much!

About the Authors

Sean Platt is an entrepreneur and founder of Sterling & Stone, where he makes stories with his partners, Johnny B. Truant, and David W. Wright, and a family of storytellers.

Sean is the bestselling author of over 10 million words' worth of books, including the Yesterday's Gone and Invasion series. Sean is also co-author of the indie publishing cornerstone, Write. Publish. Repeat. and co-host of the Story Studio Podcast.

Originally from Long Beach, California, Sean now lives in Austin, Texas with his wife and two children. He has more than his share of nose.

David W. Wright is the co-author of edge-of-your seat thrillers including the best-selling post-apocalyptic series *Yesterday's Gone*, the paranoid sci-fi *WhiteSpace* series, and the vigilante series, *No Justice*, as well as standalone thrillers *12*, and *Crash* which was recently optioned for a movie.

David is an accomplished, though intermittent, cartoonist who lives in [LOCATION REDACTED] with his wife and son [NAMES REDACTED.]

He is not at all paranoid.

He is "the grumpy one" on the *The Story Studio Podcast* with fellow Sterling and Stone founders, Sean Platt and Johnny B. Truant.

David writes about books, TV shows, movies, and

video games he enjoys; his struggles with anxiety and OCD; writing; and posts the occasional drawing at his personal blog at davidwwright.com

You can email him at david@sterlingandstone.net

We swear, he almost never bites. Unless you feed him after midnight.

For a full list of his most recent books visit sterlingandstone.net.

Also By Sean Platt

The Dead World Series

Dead Zero

Dead City

Dead Nation

Dead Planet

Empty Nest

The Beam Series

The Beam Season One

The Beam Season Two

The Beam Season Three

Robot Proletariat Series

En3my

Robot Proletariat

The Infinite Loop

The Hard Reset

Cascade Failure

Reboot

The Tomorrow Gene Series

Null Identity

The Tomorrow Gene

The Tomorrow Clone

The Eden Experiment

WhiteSpace

WhiteSpace Season One

WhiteSpace Season Two

WhiteSpace Season Three

Stand Alone Novels

Burnout

The Island

Crash

Emily's List

Pattern Black

Devil May Care

The Secret Within

Also By David W. Wright

Cold Vengeance

Cold Vengeance

Cold Reckoning

Hidden Justice

Hidden Justice

Hidden Honor

Hidden Shame

Hidden Virtue

No Justice

No Justice

No Escape

No Hope

No Return

No Stopping

No Fear

Karma Police

Jumper

Karma Police

The Collectors

Deviant

The Fall

Homecoming

Yesterday's Gone

October's Gone

Yesterday's Gone Season One

Yesterday's Gone Season Two

Yesterday's Gone Season Three

Yesterday's Gone Season Four

Yesterday's Gone Season Five

Yesterday's Gone Season Six

Tomorrow's Gone

Tomorrow's Gone Season One

Tomorrow's Gone Season Two

Tomorrow's Gone Season Three

Available Darkness

Darkness Itself

Available Darkness Book One

Available Darkness Book Two

Available Darkness Book Three

WhiteSpace

WhiteSpace Season One

WhiteSpace Season Two

WhiteSpace Season Three

Stand Alone Novels

Crash

Emily's List
Threshold
The Secret Within